THE ZACK FILES™

Trapped in the Museum of Unnatural History

LETTERS TO DAN GREENBURG
ABOUT THE ZACK FILES:

From a mother in New York, NY: "Just wanted to let you know that it was THE ZACK FILES that made my son discover the joy of reading...I tried everything to get him interested...THE ZACK FILES turned my son into a reader overnight. Now he complains when he's out of books!"

From a boy named Toby in New York, NY: "The reason why I like your books is because you explain things that no other writer would even dream of explaining to kids."

From Tara in Floral Park, NY: "When I read your books I felt like I was in the book with you. We love your books!"

From a teacher in West Chester, PA: "I cannot thank you enough for writing such a fantastic series."

From Max in Old Bridge, NJ: "I wasn't such a great reader until I discovered your books."

From Monica in Burbank, IL: "I read almost all of your books and I loved the ones I read. I'm a big fan! *I'm Out of My Body, Please Leave a Message.* That's a funny title. It makes me think of it being the best book in the world."

From three mothers in Toronto: "You have managed to take three boys and unlock the world of reading. In January they could best be characterized as boys who 'read only under duress.' Now these same guys are similar in that they are motivated to READ."

From Stephanie in Hastings, NY: "If someone didn't like your books that would be crazy."

From Dana in Floral Park, NY: "I really LOVE I mean LOVE your books. I read them a million times. I wish I could buy more. They are so good and so funny."

From a teacher in Pelham, NH: "My students are thoroughly enjoying [THE ZACK FILES]. Some are reading a book a night."

From Madeleine in Hastings, NY: "I love your books...I hope you keep making many more Zack Files."

Trapped in the Museum of Unnatural History

By Dan Greenburg

Illustrated by Jack E. Davis

GROSSET & DUNLAP • NEW YORK

For Judith, and for the real Zack,
with love—D.G.

I'd like to thank my editor
Jane O'Connor, who makes the process
of writing and revising so much fun,
and without whom
these books would not exist.

I also want to thank
Emily Sollinger and Tui Sutherland
for their terrific ideas.

Text copyright © 2002 by Dan Greenburg. Illustrations copyright © 2002 by Jack E. Davis. All rights reserved. Published by Grosset & Dunlap, a division of Penguin Putnam Books for Young Readers, New York. GROSSET & DUNLAP and THE ZACK FILES are trademarks of Penguin Putnam Inc. Published simultaneously in Canada. Printed in the U.S.A.

Library of Congress Cataloging-in-Publication Data is available.

ISBN 0-448-42632-3   C D E F G H I J

Chapter 1

If you ask me, there's something weird about museums of natural history. Whenever I go to one, lots of questions go racing through my head, like: What kind of person would want a job stuffing dead animals and putting them in those dioramas to look like they're still alive? And where do they get the people in those cave man exhibits? Were they once alive, like the animals? And when the museum closes and the lights go out, do strange things happen?

Little did I realize that I'd find out the answers to most of those questions, and sooner than I thought.

Oh, I'd better explain who I am and stuff. My name is Zack. I'm ten and a half, and I'm in the fifth grade at the Horace Hyde-White School for Boys in New York. My parents are divorced, and I spend about half my time with my dad. The events I want to tell you about started on a class trip.

Our science and homeroom teacher, Mrs. Coleman-Levin, took our class on a trip to the Rosencrantz Museum of Natural History. We were studying Neanderthal cavemen. Mrs. Coleman-Levin wanted us to see what these guys looked like.

It didn't take Mrs. Coleman-Levin any time at all to find the Neanderthal exhibit. It was behind a huge glass wall. The Neanderthal exhibit was about as long as my

dad's living room. A cave was hollowed out of a rock wall on the left side of the exhibit. We could see some kind of drawings on the walls of the cave. On the right was a big open space with scrubby bushes. On the back wall of the exhibit, a painted sun was just setting over some painted mountains.

In front of the cave, a family of Neanderthals was sitting around a campfire. The campfire wasn't a real fire. It looked like an orange lightbulb hidden under some logs. The cave family wore animal skins and no shoes. Their faces were wider than ours. Their eyes were sunk deep into their heads. Their hair was long and wild looking. They were sitting or standing kind of hunched over.

They looked like they were part human and part characters from *Planet of the Apes*. They also looked a little like Freddy the Yeti. He was a Bigfoot creature I met in the woods of Camp Weno-wanna-getta-wedgee. But that's another story.

"Who can tell me something about the Neanderthals?" asked Mrs. Coleman-Levin.

"They lived more than thirty thousand years ago," said Spencer Sharp. Spencer is the smartest kid in our class. He's also my best friend.

"Right," said Mrs. Coleman-Levin. "Thank you, Spencer. Anybody else?"

"The Neanderthals were a prehistoric people from the Late Pleistocene Period," said Vernon Manteuffel. Vernon is an annoying rich kid who sweats a lot.

"Very *good*, Vernon," said Mrs. Coleman-Levin. "How did you know that?"

"He read it off the plaque at the bottom of the glass," I said.

Mrs. Coleman-Levin sighed.

"Thank you, Zack," she said. "And what do you notice about this group in front of us?"

"It looks like they were celebrating Neanderthal Bad Hair Day," I said.

"Although the Neanderthals looked like apes," she said, "they could speak. They had their own language. They knew how to make fire and cook with it. They lived in large caves and they made paintings on the walls. Who knows what they painted on the walls of their caves?"

"Graffiti?" said Vernon.

"They made paintings of *animals* on the walls of their caves," said Mrs. Coleman-Levin. "Graceful paintings of antelopes, woolly mammoths, and saber-toothed tigers. Some say the cave paintings have magical properties. Some say the cave paintings come alive, especially during the new moon. The new moon is just the thinnest crescent you can possibly see. *Tonight* just happens to be a new moon," she said with a mysterious smile.

Some kids with cameras took pictures of the Neanderthals. Other kids made little sketches. Mrs. Coleman-Levin made all of us take notes. Then we moved on to the woolly mammoth diorama around the corner.

Woolly mammoths were huge prehistoric relatives of the elephant. They stood almost ten feet tall. They had long trunks, very long, very curved tusks, and very long, shaggy brown hair. Boy, were they shaggy! When I was young, I had a little woolly mammoth stuffed animal I slept with. I called him Fuzzy. He was cute. But these guys were scary.

"This, of course, is the woolly mammoth," said Mrs. Coleman-Levin. "Their tusks were sixteen feet long! These animals are now extinct, but they lived about the same time as the Neanderthals. In fact, Neanderthals probably hunted them for food. Not long ago, a woolly mammoth was found in Siberia, frozen in the ice."

"If it was frozen," I said, "then would the meat still be OK to eat?"

"I rather doubt it," said Mrs. Coleman-Levin. "But that's a good question."

"I had frozen woolly mammoth once," said Andrew Clancy. "It was in a Hungry Man TV dinner."

"Oh yeah?" I said. "What did it taste like?"

"It had lots of hair in it and it tasted like chicken," said Andrew Clancy. He's always making up stuff like this. Mostly nobody listens to him.

We took pictures of the woolly mammoths and made more notes.

Next we went to the saber-toothed tiger exhibit. Saber-toothed tigers had short tails and very long teeth. I mean their fangs were about eight inches long. Whew! The saber-toothed tigers lived at the same time as the woolly mammoths. So the Neanderthals must have hassled them, too.

After awhile, Mrs. Coleman-Levin looked at her watch.

"It is now nearly five o'clock, boys," she said. "The museum will be closing soon. Did you all remember to tell your parents we'll be going to dinner right after we leave the museum?"

Everybody nodded. We started making our way toward the front of the museum. I really had to go to the bathroom. Maybe I could wait until we got to the restaurant.

We passed through a large hall with a gigantic stuffed whale hanging from the ceiling. We passed through another hall that held a gigantic dinosaur skeleton. We passed exhibits of lions, tigers, grizzly bears, and wolves. We passed exhibits with great white sharks. We passed through a hall with a sixty-foot-long giant squid suspended from the ceiling. I was glad I was with my friends. If I was all alone, these exhibits would have really creeped me out.

I was looking over my shoulder, trying to decide which animal I was most afraid of, when I ran right into a man coming the other way.

"Whoops!" I said. "Sorry."

"Perhaps you wouldn't run into people if you were looking where you were walking," said the man.

The voice sounded familiar. I took a good look at the man. He was tall and thin and kind of stooped over. He had brown hair and brown eyes and brown teeth. He was smoking a pipe.

It was Professor Horatio Fufu. He's some big deal at the museum. He was really nasty to me once when I came to the museum with a live baby dinosaur I had. But that's another story.

"Hi, Professor Fufu," I said. I don't know why I said hi to him. As soon as I did, I knew it was a mistake.

Fufu leaned forward and squinted at me. Then he puffed pipe smoke in my face.

"Not *you* again," he said. "Didn't I tell you never to come back to my museum?"

"*Your* museum?" I repeated.

"Precisely," said Fufu.

"This is most certainly not *your* museum, sir," said Mrs. Coleman-Levin. "The Rosencrantz is a *public* museum."

"Allow me to introduce myself, madam," said Fufu. "I am Professor Horatio Fufu,

Head of New Exhibits, and when Mr. Rosencrantz isn't here—which he almost never is—this *is* my museum."

Mrs. Coleman-Levin snorted and hustled our class along the hallway. Professor Fufu snorted and walked the other way. I followed about ten yards behind Mrs. Coleman-Levin, looking at the animal exhibits we passed. I was beginning to think that waiting until I got to the restaurant to go to the bathroom was a lousy idea.

"Your attention, please," said a recorded voice. "The museum will close in ten minutes. Please make your way to the front lobby and the main exit doors. The museum will close in ten minutes."

I suddenly knew I couldn't wait until we got to the restaurant. I looked around for a men's room. I remembered seeing one near the hall we'd just passed through.

"Hey, guys, I'm going to the john," I called to the group ahead of me. Then I raced back to the men's room. I was pretty sure somebody had heard me.

By the time I got out of the men's room, my class was gone. I couldn't even hear their voices.

"Hey, guys!" I called. "Where are you? Spencer? Andrew? Mrs. Coleman-Levin? Hello!"

There was no answer. I started walking toward the lobby—at least I *thought* I was. It didn't look at all familiar. When I got to the end of the hallway where I thought the lobby would be, there was just another hallway.

"Your attention, please," said the recorded voice. "The museum will close in exactly sixty seconds. If you have not already left, do so immediately."

"I'm *trying* to leave!" I shouted, "but I can't find the exit!"

I wildly looked around for any kind of sign that read EXIT. There was nothing. How was I supposed to get out of the stupid museum in time if I couldn't find the stupid exit?

"Your attention, please," said the recorded voice. "The museum is now closed."

"Hey, wait a minute!" I shouted. "I'm still *in* here!"

I started running, but every hallway I ran down just led to another hallway.

"Hello!" I shouted. "Can anybody hear me? It's me, Zack! I'm lost!"

My voice echoed down the empty hallways. The museum was completely deserted.

Then the lights flickered out. I couldn't

see a thing. I was completely lost. I was all alone in the dark. I was trapped overnight in a museum full of the most frightening creatures that had ever lived!

Chapter 2

The museum was completely deserted. After a while my eyes grew accustomed to the dark. I could sort of make out shapes of things. That wasn't necessarily a *good* thing. Most of the shapes were even scarier in the dark.

The great white shark, for example. With the lights on it looked bad enough, with its rows and rows of razor-sharp teeth and its dead-looking eyes. But in the dark its eyes seemed to glow and look right at me.

Or the giant squid. With the lights on,

the sixty-foot sea creature was creepy to look at, but in the dark it looked like it was reaching its tentacles out for me.

I yelled for help a few more times. Then I stopped yelling. I guess I was afraid I might get an answer, from something I didn't want to answer me.

I passed the exhibit with the wolves and got a nasty scare. When the lights were on, the wolves had been lying down, resting. I was pretty sure of that. Now they were standing together on the other side of the glass, staring out at me.

I started walking away from the wolves, and I swear their heads followed me as I moved.

I really had to get out of this place. There had to be some kind of emergency exit. There just had to be. Yes! Up ahead was a softly glowing sign. As I got closer, I saw it said "Private. Museum Staff Only"

in lit-up red letters. I pushed hard on the door. Nothing happened. I found a door-knob and turned it. The door opened.

If the hallways were light enough to make out shapes, the room I was in now was completely black. I turned my head in all directions. When I turned completely around I saw a glow, like from a campfire. It *was* a campfire. I heard strange grunting noises. And then something grabbed me from behind!

Yikes! I practically jumped out of my skin. I started shaking like a guy breaking up the street with a jackhammer.

Whatever grabbed me was pretty strong. No matter how hard I struggled, I couldn't get away from it. I heard a whoosh, like a fire starting up, and then I saw a torch. Somebody had lit a torch and was bringing it over to look at me.

The somebody came closer. Its face

was wide and hairy and apelike. It had deep-set eyes. It was a Neanderthal! I had stumbled into the Neanderthal exhibit! Holy guacamole—the Neanderthals were alive and they'd taken me prisoner!

Chapter 3

Several Neanderthals crowded around me. They looked like they had never seen anything as weird as me before. They were really, really hairy, and they stank to high heaven. They pulled at my T-shirt. They pulled at my jeans. They shook their heads and whispered to each other. I was pretty scared.

What were they going to do to me? Serve me for dinner? Mrs. Coleman-Levin didn't say anything about Neanderthals

being cannibals. I wished I had a cell phone. I could call her and ask her if Neanderthals were cannibals.

"Hel-lo," I said slowly and clearly.

They jumped backward. I think my talking frightened them. I forced myself to smile this really fake smile.

"My...name...is...*Zack*," I said. "I...am ...a...*boy*."

The biggest one, the one who'd come to look me over with the torch, came closer.

"You not one of us," he said. His voice was kind of scratchy, kind of growly. "You speak too slow to be one of us."

"I speak slow so you can understand," I said, speaking a little less slowly. "But you're right. I'm not one of you."

"No, you from herd of animals on other side of Hard-Flat-See-Through-Thing," he said.

"That's right," I said. "I'm one of the animals on the other side of the glass. We call ourselves human beings."

"Human beans," he repeated.

"That's close enough," I said.

He suddenly grabbed the front of my T-shirt. That made me really nervous.

"Human bean, what animal this skin come from?" he asked.

"That's not an animal skin," I said. "That's called a T-shirt."

"How we can hunt T-shirts?" he asked.

"We don't hunt T-shirts, we buy them," I said.

"What means buy?"

"Buy means you give somebody money, and they give you a T-shirt."

"What means money?"

"Money is...," I said, then stopped. "OK, I don't think I have time to explain this. I have to go now. I have to go eat dinner." I acted out eating dinner.

"We have to eat dinner, too," he said. "We go out now to get food."

"You're going out to get take-out food?" I said.

"Yes, we go out now to hunt woolly mammoth, then take out meat."

"Woolly mammoths! Isn't that danger-ous?"

"Oh yes," he said. "Very dangerous. We find woolly mammoths, yell 'booga booga!' at them, try scare them to death. If we lucky we not get killed."

"That doesn't sound like such a great way to get food," I said.

He seemed hurt.

"That the Neanderthal way to get food," he said.

"Would you give it up if I can find you

other food?" I asked. "Food that tastes less hairy than woolly mammoth? Food you can get without going to all the trouble of hunting a huge, dangerous animal?"

"Where you get this food?"

"From vending machines. In the lobby."

"What means vending machine?"

"Oh, it's like this great big metal box that has food inside."

"How you get food?"

"You put quarters into the vending machine, and the food comes out."

"What means quarters?"

"Quarters are small, flat, round metal things."

The Neanderthals looked at me for several seconds, frowning. Then they burst out laughing.

"Put small-flat-round-metal-things in big box and food comes out! Ho, ho, ho! That a good one!"

"It's true," I said. "I swear it. Look, why don't you let me go now, and I'll bring back food from the vending machines?"

They whispered to each other, then turned back to me.

"What you think, we stupid Neanderthals? We let you go, you run away, we never see you again."

"No no, I'll come back to you, I promise," I said. "Look, if you don't trust me, send somebody with me."

They whispered some more. Then they turned back to me again.

"We send Moog with you," said a caveman with a gray beard. "Moog make sure you not run away."

"OK, fine," I said.

The biggest Neanderthal, the one who'd studied me with the torch, came over to me.

"Me Moog," he said.

"Oh, me Zack," I said.

I reached out to shake his hand, but he got scared and swatted at it like a cat. I pulled my hand back. They obviously didn't have the same customs we did.

Holding his torch in one hand and his spear in the other, Moog led us through a door in the painted sunset and out of the Neanderthal exhibit.

I knew I was taking a big chance. If I could get to the lobby, avoid the mammoths, find the vending machines, and bring back enough junk food, then maybe I'd be a hero. If I couldn't, then maybe I'd be a hero sandwich!

Chapter 4

Moog and I wandered through the hallways of the museum. His torch made
spooky shadows on the walls and on the
animals in the dioramas. We turned left at
the end of one hallway, then right at the
end of another, then right at the next, and
then left.

"Moog, have you ever been in these hallways before?" I asked.

Moog nodded.

"Much times," he said, "much times.
Every time there is fingernail in sky."

"Fingernail in sky?" I repeated. I had no idea what he meant. And then I got it. The new crescent moon looks a little like the end of a fingernail. And now I remembered Mrs. Coleman-Levin saying something about cave paintings coming alive during the new moon. So that must mean the creatures here only came alive once a month, during the crescent moon. I sure picked the right night to get trapped in the museum!

"Then do you know where the lobby is?" I asked.

"Lobby?" he said. "What means lobby?"

"Lobby means the front of the building, where the front door is," I said.

Moog nodded. "Then we go wrong way," he said.

He turned and started off in the opposite direction. I followed.

I wondered about my class. Did they know I was missing? Did Mrs. Coleman-Levin even notice that I wasn't with them? Why hadn't they come back to look for me? Or maybe they'd tried and they couldn't get in. Wouldn't they have called the police? Why weren't the police here now?

I thought I heard something behind me. I turned around. At first I couldn't see anything. And then I could. Behind me in the dark were about eight or nine sets of glowing eyes. Oh boy. They crept a little closer and I could make out what they were. They were the wolves!

"Moog!" I screamed.

Moog turned around. He looked at me. Then he saw the wolves.

Moog took three steps in the wolves' direction and began to growl. It was a terrible sound. Then he beat his chest with his fists and roared. The wolves turned around. They ran down the hall in the other direction, yelping in fear.

"Thanks, Moog," I said.

Moog smiled. Then we went on.

A few minutes later, we reached the front lobby. In the flickering light of Moog's torch, I found the vending machines.

"What these are?" Moog asked.

"Vending machines," I said.

Moog raised his spear and was about to hurl it at a machine.

"No, Moog!" I said. "What are you doing?"

"Kill vending machine with spear. Pull off skin. Get food."

"No no," I said. "That's not how you get food from vending machines. *This* is how. Watch."

I emptied my pockets of change. I had a bunch of quarters left over from doing

Dad's laundry. I dropped them in the machines. I bought lots of things. I bought Twinkies, Devil Dogs, and Yodels. I bought Cheese Doodles, Ring Dings, Ding Dongs, and Fruit by the Foot. I bought bottles of Yoo-Hoo and Gatorade.

Moog was amazed as each thing dropped out of the machine.

"Vending animal make babies!" he said.

"No, Moog."

"Vending animal make poopoo?"

"No, Moog."

It was hopeless to explain to him how a vending machine worked. So I didn't even try. Instead, I got him to help me carry the food back to the Neanderthal exhibit.

When we got there, all the cavemen and cavewomen crowded around us.

"Moog, what this?" asked a chubby cavewoman with a heavy moustache.

"Poopoo from vending animal," said Moog.

"This isn't poopoo!" I yelled. "This is food!" I picked up a Devil Dog and peeled off the cellophane. "Here. Taste," I said.

I held it out to the cavewoman who had asked what it was. She backed away from it.

"Look," I said. I took a huge bite out of the Devil Dog. I chewed it up and swallowed it. Then I opened a Yoo-Hoo and took a big gulp.

"What you drink?" asked a cave man with no teeth.

"Yoo-Hoo," I said.

"Hello there," said the man, "but what you drink?"

"Yoo-Hoo," I repeated.

"Yes, *hello* there, me *see* you," said the man, "but me ask what you *drink*."

"Yoo-Hoo," I said. "The name of the

drink is Yoo-Hoo. That is what I'm drinking. Do you want to taste it?"

I held it out to him. He grabbed it and stuffed it in his mouth, bottle and all. I heard crunching noises as he chewed up the glass.

"Yoo-Hoo taste good," he said. "Very crunchy."

Another caveman picked up a bottle of Gatorade.

"What is?" he asked.

"Gatorade," I said.

"Made from real gators?" he asked.

"Would you like that?" I said.

"Yes."

"Then it is."

Other cavemen and cavewomen slowly came up to us. They picked up junk food and started to eat. Some of them took the stuff out of the packages first. Some of them didn't. It didn't seem to matter. They liked whatever they ate. I ate some Yodels and a Ring Ding.

"Zack bring back good stuff from vending animal hunt," Moog said to the Neanderthals. "What we think of Zack?"

Everybody whooped and pounded the ground with their fists. That must have been the way Neanderthals applauded.

"Zack now hero of all Neanderthals!" yelled Moog.

Everybody whooped louder, and pounded the ground harder.

"Zack join tribe, become Neanderthal, too!" yelled Moog.

Everybody whooped so loud, it was frightening. And they pounded the ground so hard, it actually shook.

"Zack join Ne-*an*-der-thals! Zack join Ne-*an*-der-thals!" they chanted.

"Well, that's very nice of you," I said, "and I'm honored, I really am. But I'm afraid I can't stay and become a Neanderthal."

"Why no stay?" asked Moog.

"Because my tribe lives on the other side of the Hard-Flat-See-Through-Thing. If I don't go back to them, they will miss me. My poor father will miss me."

"Awwww," they said together.

"No want father miss Zack," said Moog. "Too sad. Make Neanderthals cry, boo-hoo." He pretended to cry.

"Well, I hate to eat and run," I said, "but if you'll just show me the way out of here, I'd better get back to my father before he cries."

I told everybody good-bye, and Moog led me out of the Neanderthal exhibit. We followed a long corridor. At the end of it, Moog pointed to a door.

"Go through this door to get to Bright-Noisy-Smelly-Place," he said.

"Thank you, Moog," I said.

I was just about to shake his hand. But then I remembered that he swatted it the last time, so I waved instead.

He waved, too. He went back to the Neanderthal exhibit.

Just as I was about to open the door to the street, it opened by itself. In came somebody I really didn't want to see—Professor Horatio Fufu.

"*You* again," he said. "Did I say I wanted you in my museum? Did I say, 'Oh, Zack, I'm so *thrilled* you came. Please stay as long as you like'? Is that what I said?"

"No," I said. "Look, Professor Fufu, I'm just leaving."

"*Are* you? Well, it's too late for that now," he said.

"Too late? What do you mean too late?"

"I mean the time for leaving was five o'clock. Closing time. It is now well past six. Besides, now you know our little secret. About what happens here every month on the crescent moon. And you'll tell everyone you know. And that will be just lovely for business, won't it? I'm sorry, my friend. You should have left when you could."

"What are you saying—you're not letting me leave?"

"I'm saying the museum is closed. Shut. Locked. Latched. Bolted. Barricaded. Sealed up. Battened down. No longer open. What part of 'closed' don't you understand?"

I tried to get past him. He wouldn't let me. He stood between me and the door.

"You know," he said, "now that I think of it, you'll fit in very nicely here. I'll make you a permanent museum exhibit. The next link in the diorama on evolution. First we have the *Rise* of Man—Neanderthal Man, followed by Cro-Magnon Man, followed by Modern Man. Then we'll have the *Downfall* of Man. You'll represent the first stage—Annoying Boy."

As he spoke, I began to hear a noise like thunder. Was it raining outside? Was there an electric storm? And then I knew what it was. The thundering noise was made by animals—animals stampeding toward us in the halls!

Fufu heard it too. He looked scared. The building began to shake.

"Oh no," he whispered.

"What is it?" I said.

"The woolly mammoths. They're stampeding again. Oh no…"

I turned around and ran. I raced down

the hallway. I didn't know which way to turn. I turned left. Maybe I should have turned right.

A thundering herd of woolly mammoths was coming right toward me—bellowing, trumpeting, stampeding! In another few seconds I'd be flatter than a soft taco shell!

Chapter 5

I spun around. I ran off in the opposite direction as fast as I could go. I could hear them behind me. I ran faster. My chest was heaving. My heart was hammering. My lungs were bursting. I knew they were gaining on me. It was no use. I couldn't outrun them. I just wasn't fast enough.

I tripped and fell hard on the hallway floor.

The instant I hit the floor, somebody swooped down and grabbed me. I felt myself flying through the air. Directly below me, woolly mammoths charged past, their sharp, curving tusks missing me by inches!

Somebody was holding me around the chest. Moog! He was swinging from something. A vine? A rope? No, it was a long electrical cord. Moog had torn an electrical cord out of the ceiling. That's what he used to save me from the woolly mammoths!

We landed on a ledge on the other side of the hallway. The woolly mammoths disappeared down the hallway.

"Moog, you saved my life!" I said. "How can I ever thank you?"

"Zack join tribe. Zack become Neanderthal, too."

"Oh, Moog," I said. "Thanks for asking. But you know I can't stay."

"Must go back to Bright-Noisy-Smelly-Place."

I nodded my head.

"No want Zack father cry, boo-hoo."

"Right," I said.

Moog thought this over. Then he nodded his head. He looked really sad.

"Follow Moog," he said.

He led the way back through the dark museum to the emergency exit. Just as we reached it, we ran into Professor Fufu. He blocked our way.

"Halt!" shouted Fufu. "Who goes there?"

"Zack and Moog," I said.

"The museum is closed," Fufu started in again.

"Have you met Moog?" I asked.

"Many times," said Fufu. "*Too* many times. But the museum is still closed. And nobody leaves!"

Moog stepped forward and bared his teeth. Fufu whimpered and raised his arms over his face to protect himself.

"Nobody leaves," said Fufu again, but not as convincingly.

Moog growled a terrible growl. Fufu screamed and ran away.

Moog opened the door. Outside I could hear the sounds of traffic.

"Well, Moog, thanks again for saving my life," I said. "I'll never forget you. So long."

"*How* long?" said Moog.

"So long. It means good-bye."

Moog looked like he was going to cry.

"Maybe Zack come back sometime and visit? Bring Cheez Doodles and Yoo-Hoo?"

"Oh, absolutely," I said.

Moog gave me a quick hug and ran away. I stepped out into the street.

Chapter 6

By the time I got to the restaurant, the kids and Mrs. Coleman-Levin had already left, so I went home.

Dad was kind of annoyed.

"It's after seven o'clock, Zack," he said. "Did dinner run late or what?"

"Not exactly," I said.

"Then how come you're so late?"

"If I tell you the truth, will you believe me?"

"You know I will," he said.

"You promise?"

"Sure."

"Well, Dad," I said. "Just as the museum was closing, I went to the bathroom. When I got out, I found out I was locked in the museum for the night. The lights went out and I stumbled into the Neanderthals exhibit.

"And, see, tonight there's a crescent moon out. And that makes strange things happen at the museum. The exhibits... well, the exhibits sort of come alive. I met some pretty nice Neanderthals. They were really hungry, so they sent Moog with me to the vending machines to buy junk food. Moog is one of their leaders and a really cool guy. He wanted me to stay and become one of the tribe, but I said I had to get back to you.

"So I tried to leave, but Professor Fufu stopped me. He wanted to stuff me and make me a permanent exhibit in the museum. But then the woolly mammoths stampeded, and I almost got trampled by them. But Moog saved me. He scared off Professor Fufu. And then I came home."

Dad didn't say a thing for a long time. Then he rubbed his eyes and sighed.

"Well, I guess that's what I get for asking," he said.

Chapter 7

At school the next day, none of the kids in my class believed my story. Mrs. Coleman-Levin didn't look like she believed me, either, but after class she took me aside.

"Tell me, Zack," she said. "Did you say you tried to shake hands with one of the Neanderthals?"

"Yes. He batted my hand away like a cat."

"And did you say Neanderthals don't applaud?"

"Right. They whoop and pound the ground with their fists."

"Just as I suspected," she said. "If you like, you can write me a report on all this for extra credit, but you must give it to me in private. And if you tell anybody I asked for it, I'll have to give you a failing grade. Do we understand each other?"

"We do," I said.

After school I met Dad at the Rosen-crantz and took him to the Neanderthal exhibit. The gang was still sitting around the campfire. The campfire was once again lit by the orange lightbulb. There was nothing at all to prove that what I'd told Dad was anything more than a truckload of horse poop.

Just as we were about to leave, I saw it.

"Hey, Dad," I said. "Check it out."

I pointed. Dad looked.

Inside the hollowed-out cave, right by the entrance, sat a crumpled-up bag of Cheez Doodles and an empty bottle of Yoo-Hoo.

Dad said that didn't necessarily prove that the Neanderthals came alive once a month. He said maybe the janitor left that stuff there or something. He also said I was probably wrong about Professor Fufu. And when Fufu threatened to make me into a permanent museum exhibit, he was probably just kidding.

Yeah, right.

Anyway, every month around the time of the crescent moon, I go back to the Rosencrantz Museum of Natural History. I leave a roll of quarters right under the window of the Neanderthal exhibit, so the gang can stock up on Cheez Doodles and Yoo-Hoo. And I always make sure I leave *before* closing time.

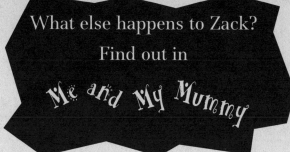

What else happens to Zack?
Find out in

Me and My Mummy

You know how sometimes when you wake up you think you're still in a dream? That's how I felt. As my eyes grew accustomed to the dark, I saw something so creepy I stopped breathing. There was somebody standing at the foot of my bed!

Oh, please, I thought, *let it be my dad!*

"Dad," I whispered, "is that you?"

There was no answer. With my heart beating in my throat, I slowly reached for the switch on my bedside lamp. I turned it on.

Yikes! Standing at the foot of my bed was the mummy!

THE ZACK FILES™

OUT-OF-THIS-WORLD FAN CLUB!

Looking for even more info on all the strange, otherworldly happenings going on in *The Zack Files*? Get the inside scoop by becoming a member of *The Zack Files* Out-Of-This-World Fan Club! Just send in the form below and we'll send you your *Zack Files* Out-Of-This-World Fan Club kit including an official fan club membership card, a really cool *Zack Files* magnet, and a newsletter featuring excerpts from Zack's upcoming paranormal adventures, supernatural news from around the world, puzzles, and more! And as a member you'll continue to receive the newsletter six times a year! The best part is—it's all free!

✂ ---

☐ Yes! I want to check out *The Zack Files*
Out-Of-This-World Fan Club!

name: _____ age: _____

address: _____

city/town: _____ state: ___ zip: _____

Send this form to: Penguin Putnam Books for
Young Readers
Mass Merchandise Marketing
Dept. ZACK
345 Hudson Street
New York, NY 10014